Ralph Waldo Emerson, Charles Eliot Norton

Letters from Ralph Waldo Emerson to a friend, 1838-1853

Ralph Waldo Emerson, Charles Eliot Norton

Letters from Ralph Waldo Emerson to a friend, 1838-1853

ISBN/EAN: 9783743335639

Manufactured in Europe, USA, Canada, Australia, Japa

Cover: Foto ©Andreas Hilbeck / pixelio.de

Manufactured and distributed by brebook publishing software
(www.brebook.com)

Ralph Waldo Emerson, Charles Eliot Norton

Letters from Ralph Waldo Emerson to a friend, 1838-1853

LETTERS

FROM

RALPH WALDO EMERSON

TO

A FRIEND

1838-1853

EDITED BY

CHARLES ELIOT NORTON

BOSTON AND NEW YORK
HOUGHTON, MIFFLIN AND COMPANY
The Riverside Press, Cambridge
1899

INTRODUCTION

THE letters and fragments of letters here printed are part of the early records of a friendship which, beginning when Emerson was thirty years old, lasted unbroken and cordial till his death. In his well-known essay, Emerson has set forth his conception of friendship in what, with no derogatory intention, he called "fine lyric words," and his idealizing genius is nowhere more manifest than in his depicting of it. For its perfection it must be free from the limitations inevitable in all human relations. It was never to be completely realized. " We walk alone in this world," he says;

"friends such as we desire are dreams and fables." But though the ideal was not to be attained, he prized, as few men have prized, the blessing of such imperfect friendship as the artificial order of society and the weakness of human nature allow to exist, and rejoiced in it as the symbol, at least, of that select and sacred relation between one soul and another "which even leaves the language of love suspicious and common, so much is this purer, and nothing is so much divine."

It is thus that his letters to his friends may show Emerson in a clearer mirror even than his poems and his essays. They are at times his most intimate expressions, the most vivid illustrations of his essential individuality, an individuality so complete and absolute as to distinguish him from all other men in his generation, and to give him place with the few of all time who have had native force sufficient to enable them to be truly themselves, and to show to their brother men the virtue of an independent spirit.

The friend to whom the letters in this little volume were addressed was younger than Emerson by nine years. At the beginning of their friendship he had lately returned from Europe, where he had spent a year and a half under fortunate conditions. Europe was then far more distant from New England than it is to-day, and more was to be gained from a visit to it. The youth had brought back from the Old World much of which Emerson, with his lively interest in all things of the intelligence, was curious and eager to learn. His own genius was never more active or vigorous, and his young friend's enthusiasm was roused by the spirit of Emerson's teaching as expressed in the famous Phi Beta Kappa discourse in 1837, the lectures on Culture, delivered in Boston in the winter of 1838, and the address before the Cambridge Divinity School in July of the same year. He did not fall into the position of a disciple seeking from Emerson a solution of the problems of life; but he brought to Emerson the highest appreciation of the things which Emerson valued, and knowledge of other things of which Emerson knew little but for which he cared much. He possessed, moreover, the practical qualities and the acquaintance with affairs in which Emerson was fortunately deficient, but which he held in high respect. I say fortunately deficient, in so far as they might have detracted from that pure idealism in which lay the unique charm of Emerson's nature, and the originality and permanence of his work.

These were happy conditions for the relation to which they led. The friends did not meet or correspond often enough to dull its edge.

C. E. NORTON.

MAY, 1899.

LETTERS

I

Miss Fuller thinks you have so much leisure, that you could come to Concord, if you would. I am particularly at leisure now, disposed to be grateful for all good influences, and especially curious of information on art and artists, of which however, I warn you, I know nothing. Will you not in these circumstances come and spend a day with me? If you are at liberty Sunday, come out here Saturday afternoon, and we will gladly keep you two nights.

R. WALDO EMERSON.

9

II

CONCORD, *August 29th,* 1839.

It is so seldom that I am in Boston with any leisure to remain, that I please myself with thinking I shall meet you at Φ. B. K. at Cambridge. Do you not go? There is a warrant for good prose and good poetry, I hope, in the names of the workmen. If you are at leisure, pray come.

R. W. EMERSON.

10

III

CONCORD, *October* 3d, 1839.

Though I hate to acknowledge times as much as Dr. Johnson did to own the existence of weather, yet it seems as if a certain perplexity were all but universal among the contemplative class of persons in this country at this moment; — the very children are infected with skepticism and ennui. Even the active, except in a very few happy instances, appear to owe their health and efficiency to their forcing the exercise of thought and the creative arts. So general a mischief will be attended by its own great advantages, and meantime the more fortunate must wait for the less with a sure trust in the remedial force of nature. To be sure, if we outgrow our early friendships there is no help, and undoubtedly where there is inequality in the intellect we must resign them, but true society is so rare that I think I could not afford to spare from my circle a poet as long as he can offer so indisputable a token as a good verse of his relation to what is highest in Being. It is possible that my love of these gifts might enable me to be useful to your friend if I knew him. As lovers of English poetry we should certainly have common ground enough to meet upon. I seldom go into company in Boston, but if I should have an opporportunity of making his acquaintance, I will not fail to use it. I shall not send you to-day Henry Thoreau's verses, but I think I shall send them soon, at least the Elegy,[1] which pleases me best.

1 This was the poem printed under the title of *Sympathy* in the volume of Thoreau's Letters, which was edited by Mr. Emerson in 1865.

IV

CONCORD, *October 27th,* 1833.

I am happy in the new relations to which you invite me by your persevering kindness. I have your portfolio [1] in my study, and am learning to read in that book too. But there are fewer painters than poets. Ten men can awaken me by words to new hope and fruitful musing, for one that can achieve the miracle by forms. Besides, I think the pleasure of the poem lasts me longer. And yet the expressive arts ought to go abreast, and as much genius find its way to light in design as in song — and probably does, so far as the artist is concerned ; but the eye is a speedier student than the ear ; by a grand or a lovely form it is astonished or delighted once for all and quickly appeased, whilst the sense of a verse steals

[1] Containing the large engravings of the ceiling of the Sistine Chapel.

13

slowly on the mind and suggests a hundred fine fancies before its precise import is finally settled.

Or is this wholly unjust to the noble art of design and only showing that I have a hungry ear but a dull eye? I shall keep your prints a little while, if you can spare them, until I have got my lesson by heart. Will you let me say that I have conceived more highly of the possibilities of the art sometimes in looking at weather stains on a wall, or fantastic shapes which the eye makes out of shadows by lamplight, than from really majestic and finished pictures.[1]

[1] This may remind the reader of the sentences in Leonardo da Vinci's *Treatise on Painting*, in which he says (I translate with some abridgment): "I will not omit from among these precepts one which, though it may seem small,. and even to be smiled at, is nevertheless of great utility in rousing the genius to various inventions, and it is this : If thou wilt look carefully at walls spotted with stains, or at stones variously mixed, thou mayst see in them similitudes of all sorts of landscapes, or figures in all sorts of actions, and infinite things which thou mayst be able to bring into complete and good form."

V

CONCORD, *November 26th,* 1839.

I confess I have difficulty in accepting the superb drawing [1] which you ask me to keep. In taking it from the portfolio, I take it from its godlike companions to put it where it must shine alone. Besides, I have identified your collection with the collector, I have been glad to learn to know you through your mute friends. They tell me very eloquently what you love, and a portfolio seems to me a more expressive vehicle of taste and character than a bunch of flowers. This beautiful Endymion deserves to be looked on by instructed eyes. But I shall not resist your generosity, and indeed am warmed at heart by your good will to me. I assure myself that we shall have opportunity of being better friends presently.

_____

[1] A copy of the antique design.

15

But I will not understand an expression of sadness in your letter as anything but a momentary shade. For I conceive of you as allied on every side to what is beautiful and inspiring, with noblest purposes in life and with powers to execute your thought. What space can be allowed you for a moment's despondency? The free and the true, the few who conceive of a better life, are always the soul of the world. In whatever direction their activity flows, society can never spare them, but all men feel even in their silent presence a moral debt to such — were it only the manifestation of the fact that there are aims higher than the average. In this country we need whatever is generous and beautiful in character more than ever because of the general mediocrity of thought produced by the arts of gain. With a few friends who can yield us the luxury of sincerity and of a manly resistance too, one can face with more courage the battle of every day — and these friends, it is a part of my creed, we always find ; the spirit provides for itself. If they come late, they are of a higher class. Of your friends I have seen two, and you have shown me the verses of another — who certainly do no discredit to your choice. In such a band I shall always be happy to be numbered.

I have copied Thoreau's Elegy that I told you pleased me so well. Some time you shall give it, if you please, to Miss Fuller. I am glad of the liberty to keep the Portfolio until after Thanksgiving.[1] I will look and see if I have any notes on any of the pictures worth sending.

[1] "I turn the proud portfolios
Which hold the grand designs
Of Salvator and Guercino,
And Piranesi's lines."

Ode to Beauty.

VI

CONCORD, *Friday eve., December* 13th, 1839.

Since you please to ask it, you shall
have the old almanac about Edmund
Burke — the only presentable piece I
find of the series. I printed two in the
North American Review.[1] It is droll to
send it to you : I dare not look into it :
but I doubt not you shall sleep the better
some night. I think I might qualify the
anodyne by sending you one of last winter's composition, a piece which I wrote
with good heart, and trust you may find
some sparks still alive in the cinders.
The argument were fitter for rhyme : but
that comes only by the special favor of
the skies. It is very pleasant to me to
write myself. . . .

R. W. EMERSON.

[1] One on Michelangelo in the number of the Review for
Jan., 1837; the other on Milton in July, 1838.

VII

CONCORD, *Friday night, January 17th*, 1840.

Read, my friend, whilst you read so well, and continue to inform me of your results. I like very well the criticism on Antigone, and perhaps shall have something to add to it by and by. Good reading is nearly as rare as good writing. I believe they are both done usually by the same persons.

Certainly we discover our friends by the very highest tokens, and these not describable, often not even intelligible, but not the less sure to that augury which is within the intellect and therefore higher. This is to me the most attractive of all topics, and, I doubt not, whenever I get your full confession of faith, we shall be at one on the matter. Because the subject is so high and sacred, we cannot walk straight up to it; we must saunter if we would find the secret. Nature's roads are not turnpikes but circles, and the instincts are the only sure guides. I am glad if you have so much patience as you say, it is the only sure method that can be trusted. If men are fit for friendship I think they must see their mutual sympathy across the unlikeness and even apathy of to-day. But I see that I am writing sentences and no letter, and as I wish you to like me, I will not add another word.

R. W. E.

VIII

CONCORD, *June 22d* [1840].

Send me, I entreat you, a particular verbal message by the bearer (for I will not ask you to write) how you do, and whether you are mending.

I am sad that you should be ill and with that ugly pertinacious ague fever; but at home you will soon throw it off. What can I do to amuse your imprisonment? Can you read? When you can, I have a precious little old book that might go in Alexander's casket with the Iliad, that I will send you to look into.

Then I am just now finishing a Chapter on Friendship (of which one of my lectures last winter contained a first sketch) on which I would gladly provoke a commentary. I have written nothing with more pleasure, and the piece is already indebted to you and I wish to swell my obligations.　　If I like it, when I read it over, I shall send it to you.

When you can write without inconvenience, send me the shortest possible note to certify me of your welfare.

R. W. EMERSON.

22

IX

CONCORD, *July 7th*, 1840.

I have delayed to thank you for the good news you sent me of your new health and strength, that I might send you the manuscript which I have set my heart on your reading. But it will not get quite finished, though I have thought it all but done, two or three times. Now will I do just what you forbid me — I will keep the paper and send the book — The Confessions of Augustine — translated two hundred years ago in the golden time when all translations seemed to have the fire of original works. You shall not be alarmed at my zeal for your reading. You shall only try your fortune in it. Some cloudy morning when you cannot ride, read twenty lines, and send it back without criticism. I push the little antiquity toward you merely out of gratitude to some golden words I read in it last summer. What better oblation could I offer the Saint than the opportunity of a new proselyte? But do not read. Why read this book or any book? It is a foolish conformity and does well for dead people. It happens to us once or twice in a lifetime to be drunk with some book which probably has some extraordinary relative power to intoxicate *us* and none other: and having exhausted that cup of enchantment we go groping in libraries all our years afterward in the hope of being in Paradise again. But what better sign can the good genius of our times show that the old creative force is ready to work again, than the universal indisposition of the best heads to touch the books even of name and fame.

R. W. EMERSON.

X

CONCORD, *July 14th, Evening,* 1840.

Your challenges are all too good to remain unanswered. I acknowledge their wit and force, and it is plain I must answer them if I can — but not now. I was so taken by the manner of the counter-statement in which too my quoted statements wore a quite Irish look, that I could not even recall the mood in which I had written or the things I had said. But though I do not much incline to compare too suddenly the statements of two parties, but rather leave each to make his own in full, sure that at last the qualification required to put it in harmony with the other and with every other will leap out, yet I have some impatience to satisfy you, as I am conscious of simplicity in these sallies of speculation. But to-night I am in no mood for writing and only wish to say how much pleasure your letter gives me, after fear for your sickness. — I have got my "Essay on Friendship" now into some shape, not yet symmetrical but approximate to that, and though it is longer than it was when I proposed to send it to you, yet it shall go. I shall not want it for some weeks.

R. W. E.

26

XI

CONCORD, *July 18th,* 1840.

The reason why I am curious about you is that with tastes which I also have, you have tastes and powers and corresponding circumstances which I have not and perhaps cannot divine. Certainly we will not quarrel with our companion that he has more roots subterranean or aerial sent out into the great universe to draw his nourishment withal. The secret of virtue is to know that the richer another is, the richer am I ; — how much more if that other is my friend. If you are a mighty hunter, if you are a Mohawk Indian with a string of equivocal, nay truculent-looking hair-tufts at your belt, if we agree well enough to draw together, those wild experiences of yours will add vivacity to the covenant. So good luck to your fishing !

The D'Orsay portrait,[1] I am sorry to say, never came. Sumner thought it was not quite ready from the printer's hand. I have sent for it since, and I hope it will arrive.

What can I tell you? Not the smallest event enlivens our little sandy village; we have not even rigged out a hay cart for a whortleberry party. If I look out of the window there is perhaps a cow; if I go into the garden there are cucumbers; if I look into the brook there is a mud turtle. In the sleep of the great heats there was nothing for me but to read the Vedas, the bible of the tropics, which I find I come back upon every three or four years. It is sublime as heat and night and a breathless ocean. It contains every religious sentiment, all the grand ethics which visit in turn each

[1] Count D'Orsay's portrait of Carlyle, which Carlyle had thought of sending to Emerson by Mr. Charles Sumner, on his return from Europe. See Carlyle's letters to Emerson in *The Correspondence of Carlyle and Emerson*, i. 299.

noble and poetic mind, and nothing is easier than to separate what must have been the primeval inspiration from the endless ceremonial nonsense which caricatures and contradicts it through every chapter. It is of no use to put away the book : if I trust myself in the woods or in a boat upon the pond, nature makes a Bramin of me presently : eternal necessity, eternal compensation, unfathomable power, unbroken silence, — this is her creed. Peace, she saith to me, and purity and absolute abandonment — these penances expiate all sin and bring you to the beatitude of the " Eight Gods."

R. W. E.

XII

This letter is just and wise and a true refreshment.   I believe I must not affect to answer it.   This is inquiry and inquirer that can never be otherwise than self-solved, and they know it very well, in what form soever they please to couch their thinking.   And yet one is tempted to say, see here again what welcome evidence to the old saw that the soul may not sleep, may not remember, but must live incessant.   Not in his goals but in his transition man is great, and the truest state of mind rested in becomes false. Our admiration accuses us.   Instead of admiring the Apollo, or the picture, or the victory at Marengo, we ought to be producing what is admirable, and these things should glitter to us as hints and stints merely.   But these beautiful modes

of the soul's expression are past — are
they? Well: Vishnu has nine or ninety
other incarnations, and is the lord of nature and is the all-excluding beauty, in
every one. I like a geranium as well as
an oak, and cannot see why every man
should not have his new and private road
into the region of beautiful production,
as well as his indisputable access, on the
other side, to the cause of causes.

Not to-day but soon I think I will
copy out of a blotted manuscript a paral-
lel text of my own to these speculations of
yours. If it should chance to be a little
too old and long it may yet lull you on
the haycock.

R. W. E.

31

XIII

CONCORD, *March 1st*, 1841.

I return Béranger and the " Letters " of Sand. I shall not, I see, read more at present in either, if I should keep them longer. I am content to accept your account of Béranger, who seems to me one who does what he undertakes ; but though we say " Well done " if we pass by, I think we should not be much the poorer if we never saw him.

I find myself, maugre all my philosophy, a devout student and admirer of persons. I cannot get used to them : they daunt and dazzle me still. I have just now been at the old wonder again. I see persons whom I think the world would be richer for losing ; and I see persons whose existence makes the world rich. But blessed be the Eternal Power for those whom fancy even cannot strip of beauty, and who never for a moment seem to me profane.

R. W. E.

XIV

CONCORD, *Monday eve., June* 27, 1841.

I thought as I walked in this amber sunset, that I would send my voice across these seventeen wide miles of hill and dale and flower-bearing fields, to say, Hail, Brother! Keep as much kindness for me in the corner of thy heart, as I hold for thee. The day will yet come when we shall celebrate it all. In truth, I am very far from consenting to be forgotten by you, and in my lonely woods I see you and talk with you so often, that it seems to me that through some of the fine channels which inform fine souls, you must sometimes feel the influence. Your frank kindness has been a bright sign in my firmament, — and few beams were ever so grateful.

You two chosen and fortunate children

33

for this present need nothing but your-
selves, and it is almost an intrusion to
come and see you, unless one can enter
gaily into the whole scenery of your en-
chanted isle.

WALDO E.

34

XV

NANTASKET BEACH, *July*, 1841.

My friend shall solve his own questions, as I suppose whoever makes a wise inquiry only announces the problem on which he is already busy and which he will be the first to dispose of, and I shall gladly attend all the steps of the solution. But is it the picture of the unbounded sea, or is it the lassitude of this Syrian summer, that more and more draws the cords of Will out of my thought and leaves me nothing but perpetual observation, perpetual acquiescence and perpetual thankfulness? Shall I not be Turk and fatalist before to-day's sun shall set? and in this thriving New England too, full of din and snappish activity and invention and wilfulness. Can you not save me, dip me into ice water, find me some girding belt, that I glide not away into a stream or a gas, and decease in infinite diffusion ? Reinforce me, I entreat you, with showing me some man, work, aim or fact under the *angle of practice*, that I may see you as an elector and rejector, an agent, an antagonist and a commander. I have seen enough of the obedient sea wave forever lashing the obedient shore. I find no emblems here that speak any other language than the sleep and aban-donment of my woods and blueberry pas-tures at home. If you know the ciphers of rudder and direction, communicate them to me without delay. Noah's flood and the striae which the good geologist finds on every mountain and rock seem to me the records of a calamity less uni-versal than this metaphysical flux which threatens every enterprise, every thought and every thinker. How high will this Nile, this Mississippi, this Ocean, rise, and will ever the waters be stayed ?

Ah ! my friend, I fear you will think that it is to little purpose that I have for once forsaken my house and crept down hither to the water side, if I have not prevailed to get away from the old dreams. Well, these too have their golden side, and we are optimists when the sun shines. I give you joy of your garden or gardenette, but I wish to know how the street and the work that is done in it look to you.

You have been here? It is a sunny breezy place with delicious afternoons and nights — to such as can be delighted. There is one person in this neighborhood whose work you ought to see, if you have not already seen them, Mr. Sprague, a house painter of Hingham, who paints birds as well as Mr. Audubon — I think, perhaps very ignorantly. I was at his house yesterday, and saw his portfolio. I shall probably go home from here or from Plymouth next Monday, and I mean to stay at home till you come and see me.

R. W. E.

XVI

CONCORD, *September 27th*, 1841. *Monday.*

We all are dressed out in tendencies, and are loved or rather tolerated for the hopes we awaken. Our children are to execute not what we foresaw, but what our best moments promised to the eyes that watched us. A fairer fortune I can hardly ask for this newest born than that she shall quickly fulfil in the common daylight the fair and religious presentiments with which her parents each and both have adorned for me some hours of solitude. So may it be and more also! And may each added hour decorate and endear the house, which, I suppose, has never before seemed lonely, but will now look so in your retrospect.

WALDO E.

XVII

In our brown lowlands, in our parti-
colored woods, the passenger finds nothing but sparrows, crows, partridges,
and though nature has no rood of meadow
so empty but to the .purged eye she can
crowd it with enchantments, — yet where
to find the euphrasy and rue that shall
make the purgation ? The laws of that
partial illumination which is permitted to
each of us, we do not know, and when
some gray rail-fence or tussuck of grass
has chanced to become a symbol to us
of things in life that are great and affect-
ing, we cannot repeat the vision or vary
the lesson. Once shut, the rock will not
open, but remains a rock. Strange magic
by which it draws us against hope to
hover and waste good time about the
same spots in the wish for new revela-

tions! But I have no secrets to tell you from the Old Mother. None have lately been told me. Lone and sad, sometimes busy and glad, I walk under this broad cope and these hospitable trees. They never seem surprised at my thoughts and seldom suffer their own to escape. Sometimes — rarely, I pity them. Often they seem to pity me. They are a great convenience, they hide and separate men who are often much better for being hid and solitary.

But how absurd to be writing to you on fields green or brown as a counterpart to your city perambulations : as if nature were less present in streets, as if the country were not too strong for the liliput interference that strives to barricade it out ; as if it did not force itself into pits of theatres and cellars of markets, as if the air, and darkness, and space and time were not nature, — wild, untamable, all-containing Nature. You and I, my friend, sit in different houses, and speak all day to different persons, but the differences — make the most we can of them — are trivial ; we are lapped at last in the same idea, we are hurried along in the same material system of stars, in the same immaterial system of influences, to the same untold ineffable goal. Let us exchange now and then a word or a look on the new phases of the Dream.

WALDO EMERSON.

41

XVIII

I was in town yesterday with the expectation of spending the night there and, in that case, of seeing you at home, but it happened that I ended my affairs faster much than I looked for, and got home here again at six o'clock, to learn that a little maiden had been here just one hour waiting to see her father. She is so quiet and contented, so incommunicable, deigning only the shortest and most unsatisfactory glances at the large and small beholders, that she interests us all, if it were only by so much majesty. And as I think that two months of growth in your babe must have quite obliterated all first impressions by so many newer and livelier, I will venture to tell you another trait of this little self-possessed and most assured personage, that she seems to me much more than a century old — say many centuries, — the hoariest antiquity, Father Apennine, or the Jungfrau Mountain not older. — So much for the little Lidian, the older one (older by the almanac) is very well and happily recruiting. The curiosity of the brother and sister is inextinguishable.

I am just announcing my new course of lectures — so far does the thirst of publishing my solitudes and the need sometimes felt by me of a stated task, add even some small degree of superstition of a necessity to speak what one fancies people ought to hear, with other reasons, drive me.

R. WALDO E.

43

XIX

CONCORD, *September 15th*, 1842.

All men, I suppose, suffer provocations, from they know not whence, to thought and to the Celestial Bounty ; but to the most it is a sting so superficial, that it blends with temperament and ends with puberty ; but when those who are more godlike hear the gods, the voices remain like the sound of the sea in the seashell, and these voices cheer them as they approach, and torment them as they depart from their true home. I suppose there are secret bands that tie each man to his mark with a mighty force ; first, of course, his Dæmon, a beautiful immortal figure whom the ancients said, though never visible to himself, sometimes appeared shining before him to others ; but, then, with scarcely less potency the vehement desires and good-will of others, expecting that of him which not his tongue but his nature promises ; and these desires flow to him often from such as cannot speak to him, and yet have the dearest interest in his success. Later, perhaps, these also become visible to him and enhance the joy of his victories.

W.

45

XX

PHILADELPHIA, *January 24th*, 1843.

I have found that I must be an absentee much longer than I thought when I saw you last, and I grow affectionate under the dispensation and write letters. You are born and bred in the world — and you probably by habit do set your expectations somewhat nearer to the mark than such persons as I, who are always victims of glare and superstition, and must continually correct our overestimates. Philadelphia, I fancied, was a great unit, a less New York, if not so large and populous, more majestic, a city of rich repose. But after conversing now with many persons here for a few days, I cannot find at all any city, any unit. A great multitude of houses, all nearly alike, lying very peacefully together, — but the tenants, from their number, very

much unknown to each other, and not
animated by any common spirit, or by
the presence of any remarkable individ-
uals. In the absence of the usual excite-
ments of trade, the whole body certainly
wears a very lymphatic appearance ; one
might call it, but for the disrespect to
the divine sex, a very large granny. For
there seems an entire absence here of
any strenuous men or man or public
opinion ; a deference to the opinion of
New York ; a fear of Boston; and, in this
great want of thought, a very dull timidity
and routine among the citizens themselves. I have diligently inquired among
the intelligent for the more intelligent ;
asked every Greek, " who was the second
best in the camp ? " yet have found no
Atrides. Very fair and pleasant people,
but thus far, no originals. If the world
was all Philadelphia, although the poultry
and dairy market would be admirable, I
fear suicide would exceedingly prevail.
I look eagerly for the stars at night, for

fear they would disappear in the dull air. I have verified the fact of a sunrise and sunset; and the sea, though in a muddy complexion, really finds its way to these wharves. When you see what facts I explore to sustain my faith, you will understand why in these extremes I should convulsively write to you, to try if the high world of man and friend still stands fast.

I must thank the Quaker City, however, for a new conviction, that this whim called friendship was the brightest thought in what Eden or Olympus it first occurred. I think the two first friends must have been travellers. — I doubt you think my practice of the *finest art* to be bad enough, but friendship does not ever seem to me quite real in the world, but always prophetic; and if I wrote on the Immortality of the Soul, this would be my first topic. Yet is nothing more right than that men should think to address each other with truth and the high-

est poetry at certain moments, far as
their ordinary intercourse is therefrom
and buried in trifles. I will try if a man
is a man. I will know if he feels that
star as I feel it ; among trees, does he
know them and they him ? Is he at the
same time both flowing and fixed ? Does
he feel that Nature proceeds from him,
yet can he carry himself as if he were
the meanest particle ? All and nothing ?
These things I would know of him, yet
without catechism : he shall tell me them
in all manner of unexpected ways, in his
behaviour and in his repose. It is time
to end my letter, yet I have only come
to the beginning of that I had to say to
you, and I think to write again presently.

Your friend WALDO E.

XXI

PHILADELPHIA, *January* 26*th*, 1843.

Before my yet libellous letter was gone to the Post Office came your letter of kind inquiries, and as I am more amiable than usual by reason of that absence I told thee of, it was very heartily received. But it shall not stop the stream of my communications on the laws of love in general and of my love in particular. I have seen lately some good people and new friendships are offered me. Then I remember the saying, that love may be increased, but not multiplied. What have I to do with you, O kind stranger? Some of the best of the children of men have put their hands into mine. I will deserve them and hold them fast. Is it not something gross to be facile to new impressions, before yet we have well established ourselves in the love of those whom we esteem? For Jean Paul says rightly "It is easy to love,— but to esteem —!" It is strange how people act on me. I am not a pith ball nor raw silk, yet to human electricity is no piece of humanity so sensible. I am forced to live in the country, if it were only that the streets make me desolate. Yet if I talk with a man of sense and kindness, I am imparadised at once. Pity that this light of the heart should resemble the light of the eyes in being so external and not to be retained when the shutters are closed. Now that I am in the mood of confession, you must even hear the whole. It is because I am so idle a member of society ; because men turn me by their mere presence to wood and to stone ; because I do not get the lesson of the world where it is set before me, that I need more than others to run out into new places and multiply my chances for observation and communion. Therefore, whenever I get into debt, which usually happens once a year, I must make the plunge into this great odious river of travellers, into these cold eddies of hotels and boarding houses — farther, into these dangerous precincts of charlatanism, namely, lectures, that out of all the evil I may draw a little good in the correction which every journey makes to my exaggerations, in the plain facts I get, and in the rich amends I draw for many listless days, in the dear society of here and there a wise and great heart. I hate the details, but the whole foray into a city teaches me much.

I have seen more of the people here. I have found out that the bay-like rivers are really rivers, and the water is not salt for twenty miles below Philadelphia, and I suppose I ought to find out that the men are. I am always sure to be shown that there is no difference in places and that the average of wit seldom varies.

WALDO E.

XXII

September 30th [1842].

Hawthorne and I visited the Shakers at Harvard, made ourselves very much at home with them, conferred with them on their faith and practice, took all reasonable liberties with the brethren, found them less stupid, more honest than we looked for, found even some humour, and had our fill of walking and sunshine.[1]

R. W. E.

[1] Mr. Cabot's *Memoir of Emerson* (p. 373) contains a fuller account of this visit to the Shakers and of the two days' walk with Hawthorne, from the record of it made by Emerson in his journal. " It was a satisfactory tramp. We had good talk on the way," wrote Emerson of it, twenty-two years later, after Hawthorne's death.

XXIII

Here are the six volumes of "Consuelo." I like nothing in the whole so well as the first volume, though there are good things in every part. The criticism on styles in art was all luminous, and the relations of art and artists to life and society are strongly sketched. Then how much the writer enjoys the bringing together of two superior persons, and painting their instant intimacy and good understanding. There is a good deal of confused and factitious matter in the Count Albert, and one wants to say to him with Dr. Johnson, "Clear your head of nonsense." No, it was Fox said so to Napoleon. And most of the characters have a dim unsubstantial look, and one fears to spy the "stars dim twinkling through their forms." Yet I think Sand shows herself to be a real person, one whose opinions will always interest you, one of the persons on the planet best worth speaking to. WALDO E.

55

XXIV

Mr. Hoar has just come home from Carolina, and gave me this morning a narrative of his visit.[1] He has behaved admirably well, I judge, and there were fine heroic points in his story. One expression struck me, which, he said, he regretted a little afterwards, as it might sound a little vapouring. A gentleman who was very much his friend called him into a private room to say, that the dan-

---

[1] Of the Hon. Samuel Hoar, and of his experience in Charleston, S. C., when sent thither as commissioner of Massachusetts, Mr. Emerson told, twelve years after the date of this letter, in a speech at Concord. It is printed in the tenth volume of his works, the volume entitled *Lectures and Biographical Sketches*. Samuel Hoar " was born under a Christian and humane star, full of mansuetude and nobleness, honor and charity ; and whilst he was willing to face every disagreeable duty, whilst he dared to do all that might beseem a man, his self-respect restrained him from any foolhardiness."

ger from the populace had increased to such a degree that he must now insist on Mr. Hoar's leaving the city at once, and he showed him where he might procure a carriage and where he might safely stop on the way to his plantation, which he would reach the next morning. Mr. Hoar thanked him, but told him again that he could not and would not go, and that he had rather his broken scull should be carried to Massachusetts by somebody else, than to carry it home safe himself whilst his duty required him to remain. The newspapers say, following the Charleston papers, that he consented to depart : this he did not, but in every instance refused,— to the Sheriff, and acting Mayor, to his friends, and to the committee of the S. C. Association, and only went when they came in crowds with carriages to conduct him to the boat, and go he must,— then he got into the coach himself, not thinking it proper to be dragged.

There was an account in the news-papers some months since of a Sheriff Batterman who was sent to serve a writ on the Rensselaer tenants in New York. I remember talking with Mr. Hoar one day, long before he was appointed to this mission, on that account. I told him I should like to give a vote for that Mr. Batterman for President of the U. S. Mr. Hoar fully entered into my respect for the officer, as indeed his own character would lead him to. He has had now a good occasion to breathe his own virtue. Our politics promise to give us fine gymnastic culture if we are inclined.

I have no literature, I believe, to offer you in return for your good news of Goethe. I read lately Alexander Henry's book of travels in America in 1766, &c. which I think the best book about the Indians I have seen. Yet I have never read Catlin. But I prize every book of facts, I believe, much more than practical men, so-called, do. Much the best

society I have ever known is a club in
Concord called "the Social Circle," con-
sisting always of twenty-five of our citizens — doctor, lawyer, farmer, trader,
miller, mechanic, &c., solidest men who
yield the solidest gossip. Harvard Uni-
versity is a wafer in comparison with the
solid land which my friends represent.
I do not like to be absent from home on
Tuesday evenings in winter.

R. WALDO E.

59

XXV

CONCORD, *February*, 1845.

Have you ever heard W. Phillips ? I have not learned a better lesson in many weeks than last night in a couple of hours. The core of the comet did not seem to be much, but the whole air was full of splendours. One orator makes many, but I think this the best generator of eloquence I have met for many a day and of something better and grander than his own.

WALDO E.

60

XXVI

CONCORD, *April* 30*th*, 1844.

The reluctant spring has yielded us some golden days and I do not know any idleness so delicious as dilettanteism in fruit trees. Grafting and pruning turn a day into pure dream, and seem to promise the happy operator a dateless longevity, inasmuch as it appears to be a suspension of all expenditure : only he must not cut his fingers.

Did you read Vestiges of Creation? I am told the journals abound with strictures, and Dr. Jackson told me how shallow it was, but I find it a good approximation to that book we have wanted so long, and which so many attempts have been made to write (by Mr. J. Herschel and Mrs. Somerville, and all the Bridgewater Treatises, &c., &c.), a digest namely, of all the recent results in all the depart-ments of Science. All the competitors have failed, and perhaps it needs a poet for a task like this, but this new Vyvyan, if it be he, has outdone all the rest in breadth and boldness, and one only wants to be assured that his facts are reliable. I have been reading a little in Plato (in translation, unhappily) with great comfort and refreshment of mind, as always happens to me in that quarter. The Correspondence of Goethe and Schiller gave me little pleasure. I shall delight to hear from you.

R. W. E.

XXVII

CONCORD, *March* 25, 1847.

I have had two letters from you which were both most welcome. You shall surely keep the books as long as you read them. We can like any book so little while! Though its pages were cut out of the sky, and its letters were stars, in a short time we cannot find there, with any turning of leaves, the celestial sentences or the celestial scents we certainly found there once; and I am of opinion that relatively to individual needs, the fiery scriptures in each book either disappear once for all from the context after a short time, or else have a certain intermittency and periodical obscuration, like " revolving lights." Perhaps too, there are cycles of epiphany and eclipse in book shops. Certainly I have seen nothing that craved to go to . . . since you gave me leave to look for you. But I shall not yet quite resign my commission.

Theodore Parker and others are considering just now, once more, the practicability of a new Quarterly Journal, and they seek for an editor. They came to me and then to C. Sumner. I promised my best help, but no editorship.[1] Sumner declined also. Then I am invited on some terms — not yet quite definite and attractive enough — to England, to lecture : in Manchester and Birmingham, and Carlyle promises audiences in London.[2] But though I often ask where shall I get the whip for my top, I do not yet take either of these. The top believes it can fly like the wheel of the Sisters, with a poise like a planet and a hum

[1] This project took form in the *Massachusetts Quarterly Review*, the first number of which, with Parker, Emerson, and J. E. Cabot as co-editors, appeared in December, 1847. It was mainly supported by Mr. Parker, and lived for three years. See *Life and Correspondence of Theodore Parker*, by John Weiss, i. 266–268.

[2] The invitation was finally accepted, and Emerson sailed for Europe in October.

like the spheral music, yet it refuses to
spin. I have read in the Cosmogonists
that every atom has a spiral tendency, an
effort to spin. I think over all the shops
of power where we might borrow that
desiderated push, but none entirely suits
me. The excursion to England and farther draws me sometimes, but the kind
of travel I should prize, the most liberal,
that made it a liberty and a duty to go, is
not to be found in hospitable invitations.
And if I could really do as I liked, I
should probably turn towards Canada,
into loneliest retreats, far from cities and
friends who do not yield me what they
would yield to any other companion, and
I believe that literary power would be
consulted by that course and not by the
public road. — When my meditations draw
to any head, I shall hasten to apprise
you, and perhaps I shall, if they do not.

Yours affectionately,

R. W. E.

XXVIII

LONDON, *March 20th*, 1848.

It was a great pleasure to see your handwriting the other day, for the first time for long. A day or two afterwards I saw Mrs. Butler, who had also news from you, which she promised to share if I would come and see her. But I fear she has already left town, and I have not used my privilege. She will quickly come back, they said. I made a point first of seeing her as Cordelia, with Macready for Lear, and I found them both excellent.

What shall I say to you of Babylon? I see and hear with the utmost diligence, and the lesson lengthens as I go ; so that, at some hours, I incline to take some drops of or grains of lotus, forget my home and selfish solitude, and step by step establish my acquaintance with Eng-

lish society. There is nowhere so much
wealth of talent and character and social
accomplishment, every star outshone by
one more dazzling, and you cannot move
without coming into the light and fame
of new ones. I have seen, I suppose,
some good specimens, chiefly of the lit-
erary-fashionable and not of the fashion-
able sort. Macaulay is quite the king of
every circle where he goes, by the splen-
dor and the speed of his talking. He
has the strength of ten men, I may well
say, and any table-talk of his is an ex-
ploit to found a reputation on. Mr. Hal-
lam is affable, but comparatively quiet.
Bunsen is reputed a man of learning and
wide information and is much a man of
society, but he talked little when I saw
him. Milnes is the most gentle friendly
all-knowing little-caring omnipresent person that can be. You see him so often
that you think it must be Boston, not
London. Lord Morpeth's virtues give
him the highest consideration, both in

public and in private circles. Mr. Charles
Austin is a lawyer of great reputation,
and of special talent that makes him
the only fit match for Macaulay. Milman is a very polished man and Mrs.
Milman a superior woman, and they are
the centre of a distinguished circle. Carlyle does not very often dine out or go to
breakfasts, so that I do not well know
how he, who is a wonderful talker, man-
ages his tomahawk among these Romans.
I have seen also Lady Harriet Baring,
esteemed the wittiest woman in London,
and am to dine with her this week, — a
lady in great respect. Kinglake I have
seen, a sensible man enough, but he does
not look the Eothen ; and Barry Corn-
wall, at whose house I found him and
Thackeray, you should never mistake for
a poet. They have all carried the art
of agreeable sensations to a wonderful
pitch, they know everything, have everything, they are rich, plain, polite, proud
and admirable. But though good for

them, it ends in the using. I shall or should soon have enough of this play for my occasion. The seed-corn is oftener found in quite other districts. But I am very much struck with the profusion of talent which allows everybody to be ignorant of the authors of paragraphs, articles and books, which all read with admiration, but have not any guess of the writer. Tennyson, whom I wished to see more than any other, is in Ireland, and I fear I shall miss him. I saw Wordsworth to very good purpose in Westmoreland, and all the Scottish gods at Edinburgh. Perhaps it is no fault of Britain, — no doubt it is because I grow old and cold,— but no persons here appeal in any manner to the imagination. I think even that there is no person in England from whom I expect more than talent and information. But I am wont to ask very much more of my benefactors, — expansions that amount to new horizons. But this is very idle gossip, and when I come home,

I will mend it by giving you all my impressions of this fine people — if I can remember them. Meantime do not fail to write me immediately.[1]

R. W. EMERSON.

[1] Much of the contents of this letter may be found developed in Emerson's *English Traits*. The contemporaneously recorded impressions were but little modified by retrospection.

XXIX

At Sea [on the homeward voyage].
                Steamship EUROPA, *July 22d*, 1848.

The daily presence and cheerful smiles
of your brother make it almost impera-
tive, if I had not besides a just debt, to
write you a page, and it will be some
sunshine in these head winds and long
disgust of the sea, to remember all the
gallery of agreeable images that are wont
to appear with your name.   What games
we men so dumb and lunatic play with
one another !   What is it or can it be to
you that through the long mottled trivial
years a dreaming brother cherishes in a
corner some picture of you as a type or
nucleus of happier visions and a freer
life.   I am so safe in my iron limits from
intrusion or extravagance, that I can well
afford to indulge my humor with the
figures that pass my dungeon window,

without incurring any risk of a ridiculous shock from coming hand to hand with my Ariel and Gabriel. Besides, if you and other deceivers should really not have the attributes of which you hang out the sign, you were meant to have them, they are in the world, and it is with good reason that I rejoice in the tokens. Strange that what is most real and cordial in existence should lie under what is most fantastic and vanishing. I have long ago found that we belong to our life, not that it belongs to us, and that we must be content to play a sort of admiring and secondary part to our genius. But here, to relieve you of these fine cobwebs, comes an odd challenge from a fellow passenger to play chess with him; me too, who have not played chess, I suppose, for twenty years. 'Tis of a piece with the oddity of my letter, and I shall accept that, as I write this. Shadows and shadows. Never say I did it. Your loving fellow film.

XXX

SEA WEEDS. — Two very good men [1]
with whom I spent a Sunday in the country near Winchester lately, asked me if
there were any Americans, if there were
any who had an American idea? or what
is it that thoughtful and superior men
with us would have? Certainly I did not
retort, after our country fashion, by defy-
ing them to show me one mortal Eng-
lishman who did not live from hand to
mouth but who saw his way. No, I assured them there were such monsters
hard by the setting sun, who believed in
a future such as was never a past, but
if I should show it to them, they would
think French communism solid and practicable in the comparison. So I sketched

[1] These two good men were Carlyle, and Mr. (afterward
Sir Arthur) Helps. The conversation is recorded in *English Traits*, ch. xvi.

73

the Boston fanaticism of right and might without bayonets or bishops, every man his own King, and all coöperation necessary and extemporaneous. Of course my men went wild at the denying to society the beautiful right to kill and imprison. But we stood fast for milk and acorns, told them that musket-worship was perfectly well known to us, that it was an old bankrupt, but that we had never seen a man of sufficient valor and substance quite to carry out the other, which was nevertheless as sure as Copernican astronomy, and all heroism and invention must of course lie on this side. 'T is wonderful how odiously thin and pale this republic dances before blue bloodshot English eyes, but I had some anecdotes to bring some of its traits within their vision, and at last obtained a kind of allowance; but I doubt my tender converts are backsliding before this. — But their question which began the conversation was so dangerous that I thought of no escape but to this extreme and sacred asylum, and having got off for once through the precinct of the temple, I shall not venture into such company again, without consulting those same thoughtful Americans, whom their inquiry concerned. And you first, you who never wanted for a weapon of your faith, choose now your colors and styles, and draw in verse, or prose, or painted outline, the portrait of your American.

Forgive these ricketty faltering lines of mine; they do not come of infirm faith or love, but of the quivering ship.

Ever your friend,

R. W. E.

75

XXXI

CONCORD, *July 12th*, 1849.

The Club is not so out at elbows as your friend fancied, for besides other good men whom I do not remember, Cabot was there, who is always bright, erect, military, courteous and knowing, a man to make a club. Then Hillard, Lowell, Longfellow, and other men of this world, have all shown themselves once — and, with a little tenderness and reminding, will all learn to come. There is a whole Lili's Park,[1] also with tusks and snakes of the finest description. Belief is the principal thing with clubs as well as in trade and politics. And really we have already such good elements nominally in this, that the good luck of

1 " Lili's Park " is a half-humorous poetic autobiographic allegory of Goethe's, in which he represents himself as the bear in subjection to Lili's charm.

a spirited conversation, or one or two happy rencontres would now save it. Henry James of New York is a member, and I had the happiest half hour with that man lately, at his house, so fresh and expansive he is. My view now is to accept the broadest democratic basis, and we can elect twenty people every month, for years to come, and yet show black-balls and proper spirit at each meeting.

R. W. Emerson.

77

XXXII

The Horticultural paper never came, and I am left to guess your opinions on Downing. Do not fail to inquire on your side, for my postmaster is positive here. — I send you, I am ashamed it is so late, with Dr. Carlyle's compliments, a copy of his Dante.[1] The Doctor's presentations are slow, fault of the Harpers, who forget their author for a time. But the book is worth waiting for, the most conscientious of translations. Confirm me, if you can, in my estimate of it. I read it lately by night, with wonder and joy at all his parts, and at none more than at the nerve and courage which is as essential to poet as to soldier. Dante locked the door and put the key in his pocket. I believe, we value only those who do so.

R. W. E.

[1] Dr. John Carlyle's excellent translation of the *Inferno*, published in this country by Harper & Brothers.

XXXIII

I saw Longfellow at Lowell's two days ago, and he declared that his faith in clubs was firm. "I will very gladly," he said, "meet with Ward and you and Lowell and three or four others, and dine together." Lowell remarked, "Well, if he agrees to the dinner, though he refuses the supper, we will continue the dinner till next morning!" — Meantime, as measles, the influenza and the magazine appear to be periodic distempers, so, just now, Lowell has been seized with aggravated symptoms of the magazine, — as badly as Parker or Cabot heretofore, or as the chronic case of Alcott and me. He wishes to see something else and better than the Knickerbocker. He came up to see me. He has now been with Parker, who professed even joy at the prospect offered him of taking off his heavy saddle, and Longfellow fosters his project. Then Parker urges the forming of a kind of Anthology Club[1]: — so out of all these resembling incongruities I do not know but we shall yet get a dinner or a "*Noctes.*"

Ever yours,

R. W. E.

[1] The Anthology Club was a club of men of letters which had existed in Boston in the early years of the century. Emerson's father was one of its members, and editor for a time of the journal, *The Monthly Anthology*, from which the club took its name.

XXXIV

CONCORD, *November 22d*, 1853.

My little household is grown much less by the loss of my Mother. She was born to live. She lived eighty-four years, yet not a day too long, and died suddenly and unexpectedly at the last. She was born a subject of King George, was bred in the Church of England, and, though she had lived through the whole existence of this nation, and was tied all round to later things, English traditions and courtesies and the Book of Common Prayer 'clung to her in her age, and, had it been practicable, it would have seemed more fit to have chanted the Liturgy over her, and buried her in her father's tomb under Trinity Church.[1]   R. W. E.

[1] In Mr. Cabot's *Memoir* of Emerson (p. 572) is a letter to his brother William, three days earlier in date than the preceding, which contains similar expressions concerning his mother's death. " Her mind and her character were of a superior order, and they set their stamp upon manners of peculiar softness and natural grace and quiet dignity." *Ibid.*, p. 37.

www.ingramcontent.com/pod-product-compliance
Lightning Source LLC
Chambersburg PA
CBHW032356020726
47499CB00008B/2776